# MARTIN ROWE

## MEMORIAM

*100 Poems* (1918 – 2018) *100 Years*

.

*Dedicated to that lost generation,*

*Lest we forget.*

# *Contents*

# I Flinch

When shells shriek their shrill songs,
Smashing together earth and sinew,
To form foul cascading plumes.

I flinch.

When gas grabs at gasping guys,
Filling lungs with filthy fluids,
And melting sight from sorest eyes.

I flinch.

When wires wrap around war willed,
And string up their convulsing bodies,
For the sport of statesmen and snipers.

I flinch.

When moans court the midnight moon,
Crying tortured souls across,
The hell of no man's land.

I flinch.

When haggard hands hasten lice,
From clothes and crude crevices,
As fevered poxes turn flesh to stone.

I flinch.

When brass bugles instruct British bodies,
To dodge the mines and cut the wire,
In the name of the shilling king.

I flinch.

When whistles will the withdrawn,
To stumble out of their trench, and mind
The coming bullets.

I flinch.

When privates pray for protection,
Promised by strutting peacocks,
As men march to bits.

I flinch.

But when darling death's sweet caress,
Drives out the dark from my being,
Ending this devilish misery,

I flinch no more.

# Gas!

Gas – Panic! Gas – Panic!
Bodies flail fumble frantic.
Breathing races.
Hearts stop.

Then through my dim windows,
I see tendrils of yellow,
Seeping and hissing.
A serpent of mists.

Muffled cries. My cries,
Fingers claw at eyes.
Burning. Burning.
Its sweet smell sickly – suffocating.

I rip off the mask.
A warm breeze washes my face.
A corrosive wind that rubs sores into skin,
Weeping raw and dying.

Gas – Panic! Gas – Panic!
Silhouettes stumble to my side.
Men fussing and frightened,
Their faces peer down behind unnatural
panes.

In which I see my reflection.

A blistered mess, vile and vulgar,
Shivers in a sea of yellow.
Gasping for air,
Clutching at life.

Chunks of bloody vomit then,
Snatch away my breath,
The world spins,
I fall.

Gas – Panic! Gas – Panic!
Nurses dab my brow and fidget about me.
I scream whispered whimpers,
My voice stolen in the fog.

Faces smile but long to look away,
As my eyes stick,
And blisters burst their hot fluids.
My body seeping into sheets.

Doctors poke and prod,
And tut at spoilt meat,
Covering what remains,
In a crypt of linen.

Left to some forgotten corner.
To die.
I rest in the jaws of agony,
As my sight leaks from septic eyes.

Gas – Panic! Gas – Panic!
My throat closes. Lungs burnt away,
Muscles tighten –
Drowning, drowning –

Drowning in a frothy fountain,
That spills from my mouth,
As blood and waste and life,
Oozes from offensive orifices.

And so I gasp.
And grab.
And clutch, and scratch, and claw, and cry –
But it's no use.

For I have left my breath in the trenches.

# Doves of Glass

Shadows slouch in sludge.
Broken husks.
Empty.

"Quick lads!" a voice calls.
Limbs fumble.
Muscles scream.

Men emerge from their filth,
Of mud and rats and war,
And stand to attention. Blank faced.

Silence comes over them,
Despite the screaming shells,
And the chatter of guns.

The stranger arrives then,
Preened in khaki green,
Clean and tainted.

He parades in front of skeletons,
Fat wobbling. Nose wrinkling.
Eyes blinded to his sights.

The men line their trench.
Bodies betraying minds,
That drown in nightmarish seas.

He ruffles hair with soft hands.
Offers empty words.
A sheep among lions.

And when he reaches the end of the line.
Such a small line.
His gaze rests on Tommy.

The soldier leans on busted legs.
Body bruised and beaten.
Yet he stands.

He stands as the stranger smiles his
warmless smile,
On a face fake and forged,
That flinches at the fires of war.

But men look on.
Numbed to familiar horrors.
Filthy forsaken figures.

The sheep looks into the eyes of Tommy
then.
Empty pools in sunken pits.
And sees the lion's pain.

And in that moment,
The general understands,
As tears fly from his eyes like doves of
glass.

# Oh Pigeon!

Oh pigeon! What hells await you,
*As you fly.*
Fly from our fields of slaughter.
What scenes you shall survey,
*As you flee.*
Flee through the iron dome of propellant and
metal.
What awful spectacles you shall witness,
*As you flutter.*
Flutter in the unnatural sea of toxic fumes
and final breaths.

Oh pigeon! How I pity you.
As you dodge the shells that plague our
skies,
Like a weeping pestilence of the heavens.
Sent from our earth scorched and pitted,
That drinks deeply from septic pools,
And the mulch of festering flesh.

And as you bravely flit through this cesspit
of wastes most foul,
Do not look upon the armies of the damned,
As they feign fearlessness,
And lob their bombs,
And stab with sharpened sticks,
In the name of a cause that sits behind them,

Where the world is green and sane.
For you will fall. As we have all fallen.

Oh Pigeon!
Fly as you soar,
Over sores opened by suits seated in
ignorance.
For on your feathered wings rests our hope,
That we forlorn few might be saved,
As we lie here beyond the wire,
Courting our madness and death.

Oh Pigeon!
What hells await you as you fly.

# The Cold Light of Stars

Under the cold light of stars,
Shadows sit huddled,
Coughing and hacking at life,
With failing lungs and minds,
That long to go inside.
Cigarettes glow in the night,
Dim dots of orange,
That send wisps of life from the trenches.

Some men drift into a wakeless sleep then,
Comforted by the stillness of the night.
That odd interval between two demented
acts,
Doomed to irreversible repetition,
Like the souls that succumb to unspeakable
scenes,
Day after day after day…

Black clouds drift past a lonesome moon,
Pale and uncaring its light bathes the scars
that cut into the earth below.
Illuminating lines and fissures and crude
crags,
That hide festering figures in the deep spoil
of the front.

Over the top of trenches,

Wire sprawls across cratered wastes,
That flow with mud clogged pools of blood
and flesh.
Corpses lie here as carrion,
Primed to be picked to pieces by morning
crossfire.
Some still groan as death's rattle chatters
their teeth,
And drains life from open wounds and
limbless holes.
Damned to the same fate as the branchless
trunks,
That stand like decayed watchmen of the
deceased.
Tombstones marking the fall of man and his
kind.
Dying horses lie here too with their masters,
With both crying out for death,
And both being made to wait.
And so they wait, as equals before their end.

Further out across this glorious field,
Beyond another scattered wire that shreds
dispirited souls,
As convulsing bodies sway on its barbed
string,
There lie more deep cracks in the earth's
great crust.
Wrinkles as old as time.
Vast and unnatural.

These ditches burst with the diseased and
dying.
The children of war.
Whose screams for death and laments for
home,
Drift to the heavens,
Yet the heavens look on.
As the cold light of stars,
Fade with the first light of morn…

*And so goes the dawn chorus,*
*Of guns.*

# Their Wasteland

Across the poisoned fields,
Scattered brown and barren,
Sprout dead things that blossom in decay.
Lifeless stumps stand diseased and rotten,
Trees once, stripped by artillery and gas,
That drink from stagnant streams of corpses
juices,
And bathe in acidic rains.

Pools and puddles of venoms and poxes
corrupt this earth,
A scourge of life in the mud,
That squelches into anaemic sludges and
foulest froths.
Dismembered limbs and faded eyes,
Rest restless in this filth.
Pale and dead and decomposing remains,
That haunt the land. Poor pitiful souls,
Whose numbers are bolstered as the earth
purges bodies,
From deep set trenches day after tedious
day.
Cast out like maggots exploding from
infected wounds,
To die and join the bits of their brothers,
That lie dissolving into septic slimes.

Even the air that is filled with fetid fumes,
Sings with screaming shells and shrapnel,
That bury into flesh and earth,
And shred both just the same.
While wires barbed and rusted,
Drip with blood and bloated bodies,
That ooze and fester,
As men huddle in ditches and dugouts.
Contemplating their fate in this,
Their wasteland.

# Mud

Hot summer rains sweep over us,
Swelling earth into corrupting torrents,
That lap foul filth at our knees.
Its putrid smell teases vomit from empty
stomachs,
Adding bullied beef and spoilt tea to the
rancid soup.
Yet we press on, and wade with heavy legs
and hearts,
Through the sludge and waste.

Soon we turn the corner of this forsaken
ditch,
Feet slipping on drowned duckboards,
Until we come to it then,
A collapsed trench streaming all the fluids
of no man's land,
Into out frontline home.

As we get closer I can see that there is more
than earth to this earthy mess,
For fingers pale and gangrenous stick out at
peculiar angles.
Some scolding the heavens,
Some pointing at me as if to say through
lipless mouths,
"We are one of the same."

A coldness comes over me then,
As I reach for my spade and dig.
The others shift the soil fast at first,
But when their shovels fill with jellied flesh,
And hands and fingers and toes,
They recoil in disgust dry heaving.

I wretch then as my spade hits and screeches
its strike on bleached bone,
Part of a skull blown to pieces by that
mortar,
Though its one remaining eye socket,
Empty and dark,
Follows my every effort to clear its grave.

I dig deeper with spade and mind,
As sinister scents escape the spoil,
Offensive odours that should be left buried,
Follow men like warped muses that whisper
sick memories of their hell –

"Come on!" I shout through my damp
sleeve.

Hours pass before we clear the mound of
fleshy bits and dirt,
With spades and shovels and my hands,
Now tainted and unclean,
For my shovel had snapped when it snagged
on submerged wire,

And so I plunged my calloused hands into
the filth,
And wriggled my fingers along the hungry
barbs,
So that my blood oozed into its bloodthirsty
depths.

I pulled my hands out then,
Eyes surveying the gashes that leaked
crimson rubies,
Over trembling fingers and shaking wrists
and into the mire.
I tried to wash the brown away,
But it sticks to my skin like war paint.
A plague of the warring.

And so as the rains give way to a sticky
dusk,
We turn back and wade through the
putrescent floods,
While I struggle to scrub my hands slick
with mud,
That foulest of matter,
In which we few live,
And die.

# Censor

I sit here and censor,
Countless letters and words,
That talk of a foreign war,
In a foreign field,
In a foreign land,
And yet I'm the foreigner.
For my eyes have stolen the stinging meaning,
Etched in shaking ink,
By men whose frail hearts and desperate minds struggle,
To make sense of it all.

I sit here and censor,
Alone save for the countless voices,
That echo from the pages,
That lie before me like an opened corpse,
Whose entrails are laid bare for the distressing task,
Of tidying the torso, sewing back limbs, closing the wounds –
My honourless work that does not console my heart or mind,
As I drown in the sea of my shame.

I sit here and censor,
And rob men dead and living,

Of their words and thoughts.
With each crude stroke of black,
I steal away that last bit of humanity that
keeps out the animal.
I hide secrets from their mothers.
I delude fathers.
And I lie to their sweethearts and children,
Who sit nestled in secluded shires,
Believing in a Christmas that passes each
year with nothing but news of the dead,
And dying.

I sit here and censor,
And weep as I work.
Condemning words and writing to the black.
Never to whisper secrets to aching hearts,
Never to be read by long forgotten eyes,
Never to reach home.
That place all men hold dear as they writhe
about in their waste.
For many a fatal delusion as they reach for
their grave,
That they have been read and remembered.
Another great lie offered to the children of
this Great War.
Who sit huddled with rats,
And treated just the same.

Oh how I weep,
As I sit here,

And censor.

# Blind

We were led into darkness.
A line of brothers guided by strangers,
Who offered us cheerful talk of Blighty,
Despite the blight that oozed from our
sockets.
We sheepishly walked forwards,
Broken men lost in their nothingness.
Hands on shoulders, hearts in mouths,
Stumbling over the mire of corpse and mud
and decay,
To rest in comfort offered by disembodied
voices,
That pass over us like the wind,
That stole the light from our world.
Here days and nights merge together
unbroken,
Save for the voices that push for sleep –

*But how can I sleep?*

For when I wake I shall not see the sun.
I shall never again see the distant stars,
Or the pale face of the moon.
For I am abandoned to a dark that has
eclipsed my mind,
And smothered that smallest ember of hope,

That I might survive and see this world
again.
But now such hope has diminished into a
familiar shadow,
My eternal torment.
For I now live in the black of my head,
That haunted tomb of memories,
Where restless ghosts call my name,
Until I surrender…

For I am blind.

# Glory of War

A lie lied by liars,
Whose blind eyes fell on butchered boys in
battle,
Oh how they preached of King and Country!
And lured loved ones into war lusts,
Sowing their seeds of hate.
Oh how they trumpeted with bugle brass,
Their deceits and delusions,
That unleashed ditches and devils upon a
world,
That slept in ignorance,
Through the slaughter.
Oh the shame.

A myth muttered by murderers,
Who turned their backs on the dead,
That marched to their orders and fell
frightened in Flanders mud,
As worthless numbers,
Nameless fodder.
Cast into a breathing hell to die,
In spirit,
And mind,
And body.

A fiction fed by familiar foes,
Who dressed in flags,

And called for their nation's sons to stand,
And salute,
And sit in foul fields,
To be broken by shells and scenes,
And walked into gunfire and mines,
That locked away their souls,
In their eternal silence.

But if these liars and murderers and foes,
Could look up from their papers and maps
and plans,
And gaze upon their front,
They would find it hard to sing with dry
eyes and impassioned tones,
That old song,
That warped warble,
Their song,
Of the glory of war.

# Vaulted Halls

Hear how the guns echo down the vaulted
halls of history,
And how the screams and cries rise and fall,
Like the dying breaths of their hosts,
Who like shadows dance in the sepia of our
past.
Hear too the chilling silence of loss,
That seeps grief into the walls and columns,
And steals away warmth from the dim light,
That illuminates this tomb of war.
But the forgetful have forgotten,
And sowed their weeds amongst poppies,
Into cracks that threaten ruin to memorials,

And memories,

And minds.

For tomorrow's war echoes here,

In our vaulted halls,

Of history.

# Poppies

Red fields blossom into red fields.
Blood red petals swaying,
In the autumnal breezes that whisper,
Of a recent storm.
Whose angry clouds rest black and
foreboding on the horizon,
Threatening their return,
Over poppies most read that grow in silence.

Elegant.

Graceful.

Dignified.

And whose fragile roots are anchored in
waste,
That feed their bursting buds,
And swell this sea of red.
A blanket to comfort the fallen,
As they rest restless in their graves.

# 'The Great War'

As soon as the guns cooled in their silence,
And the shells left the sky to the birds,
And the bullets lay dormant in their barrels,
And corpses were buried or marched home,
And fields drank of water not blood,
And poppies bloomed as people sighed,
And fevered nations recovered from fevers,
And priests mouthed their silent prayers,
And politicians offered their empty words,
And nurses nursed their memories,
And soldiers mourned their mates and
minds,
And families survived minus one,

Or two,

Or three…

And remembrance taught how to forget,
And the fogs of peace softened the horrors,
And sowed the seeds of ignorant illusions –
Vacant voices clambered to proclaim,
That war of 1914,

As 'The Great War'

…

# Shellshock

That faraway look,
That lock poor men,
Inside their heads.
Forced to faraway places,
Beyond sense or reason.
Unreachable, untouchable, unbearable.
And in whose vacant eyes,
Their fleeting souls do scream,
And echo in echoless silence.

That faraway look,
That lock poor men,
In lives that died,
As shells burst their ears,
And shredded their spirits,
And scarred sick smiles,
On their frightened faces.
Pale and cold,
And lost.

That faraway look,
That lock poor men,
Outside of themselves,
Forced to peer through storms of madness,
That swirl in bruised skulls,
Their silent tempest of unthinkable hells,
That frighten them from their minds.

# Whistles

Shrill whistles sound dread,
To men dreading their demise.
That unnatural tune and metallic screech,
Send jitters and jangles,
Down trenches and ditches,
Where the damned nurse their nerves.

Shrill whistles sound death,
To men awake and alarmed,
To the horrors that await them,
Over the top and across the mire,
In which no man lives to tell their tale.

Shrill whistles sound fear,
To men at the foot of ladders,
Whose feet freeze on rungs,
Despising that whistled signal,
Shrieking in the silence of guns,
To attack.

# The Wire

Sprawling lines lie sprawled.
A stinging mass of iron,
That rusts in blood and rain.
Fresh and putrid bodies,
Swing and hang on its barbs,
As scarecrows to the living,
And carrion to the crows.
Their limbs caught,
Skin slashed and sliced,
Flesh ripped and snagged,
On metal thorns,
That cut across the fields,
And cut into men,
As they march through the mud,
To tangle with the wire.

# Trench Foot

My feet have drowned,
In still puddles and stagnant lakes.
Bogged down by bogs,
And marshes of the mad.

My toes have swollen to gangrenous stumps,
Black. Green. Putrescent.
In which nails have abandoned their host,
And skin has peeled away from fruits of
flesh,
To unlock unholy aromas,
And decay that drips from rotting bones,
Dissolving in this damned damp.

Agony nags away at me from within my
boots.
Nibbling and gnawing at my sores.
Gnashing teeth cruel and crude devour my
feet.
An unseen weapon,
That feasts on our flesh,
And my soul,
In slow and steady and stationary bites.
Wounding. Maiming. Crippling.

"You've got trench foot," they tell me.
"I might as well be dead," I reply.

So as bits of my feet bury into mud,

I bury a bullet in my head.

# Flares

Like shooting stars,
Flares climb to the heavens,
And burst into merciless light.
Chasing away the dark,
To reveal the dark that blights men's lives,
And darkens their doorways and hearts.

Like shooting stars,
Flares climb to the heavens,
And burst into merciless light.
As fleeting as our hope,
That rests under shadow,
That blackest of curses,
That rob men of life,
Women of spirit,
Children of future.

Like shooting stars,
Flares climb to the heavens,
And burst into merciless light.
That illuminates the worst in mankind,
War.
That blights our lives,
And darkens our doorways and hearts.

# Panic!

Panic – Gas! Panic – Gas!
Limbs flail fumble frantic,
Breathing races,
Hearts stop.

Men carry men to their beds,
Bodies burned and blistered.
Wounds staining sheets,
Eyes streaming sight.

I tend to them then.
A nurse faking calmness,
As I soothe their distress,
With pitiful lies of kindness.

Panic – Gas! Panic – Gas!
They call out to their mothers,
Those brothers and husbands and sons.
Lost boys.

I hold their withered hands,
And ease them from their minds,
With cheerful talk of Blighty,
Despite their stench of death.

Some are blinded to their plight,
As they writhe about in darkness,

*Poor pitiful chaps,*
*It won't be long now.*

Panic – Gas! Panic – Gas!
I see him then,
Through the blur of my tears,
And sanity.

He lies on his back,
Screaming at the heavens,
Eyes white with fearful rage,
Mouth open. Soundless.

I rush to his side,
My eyes avert his body,
That rests writhing and twisting,
Wracked with agony.

Panic – Gas! Panic – Gas!
*Shh!* I plead with him,
And he obliges,
As he clutches at his neck.

He digs his hands into his flesh,
Gurgling and gargling liquid gas,
As frothy blood and putrid pus,
Leak from his mouth.

I wipe it away,
And try to help.
But I am helpless,

And he is beyond help.

For he has left his breath in the trenches.

# Buried

I lie here buried under the weight of war.
Earth presses breath from my body,
And extinguishes light from the hope,
My hope,
That I might live.
That I might claw my way from the dark.
That I might breathe and save myself –
But my soul is beyond salvation.
For I have seen too much,
Heard too much,
Done too much.

And so when the howitzer howled its arrival,

I did not fear.

I did not feel.

For long have I laid buried under the weight
of war.

# That Fabled Night

Silent night whispered through the silent
night,
That fabled night.
Festive spirit silenced the guns,
That fabled night.
When boys put down their weapons,
That fabled night.
And remembered they were human,
That fabled night.
So both sides went over the top,
That fabled night.
And greeted under the starlight,
That fabled night.
And joked and shook hands and made small
talk,
That fabled night.
And played that beautiful game,
That fabled night.
And shared a smoke and a smile,
That fabled night.
In which the war stopped for breath,
That fabled night.
Before the madness that followed,
That Christmas Eve night, 1914.

# Smoke and Mirrors

Shells burst about me.
Bullets whizz past.
A stalking death,
That casts shadows across my path.
I crawl into a crater then,
Safe but for the German who aims a
revolver at my skull…

Our eyes meet…

Enemies face the mirror.

His pale face looks worn,
Withered by the elements and the slaughter.
Eyes dead save for their slow blink.
A shell breaks the moment,
And showers us with cascading earth.
I wrestle with the chaos.

Another shell greets us…

My mind whirls.
Body flung across the crater.
Ears blown,
Deaf but for the ringing raging in my
mind…

I feel the revolvers cold touch against my
temple.
I gulp, eyes closed to their fate.
But he grabs my shirt then,
And pulls me to the craters edge...


"Kill me," the words betray my lips.

I peer into his face then,
He is young. Younger than me,
A younger me.
"Kill me," I groan ill-disguised secrets of
my exhaustion...

Our eyes meet...

Enemies face the mirror.

But upon seeing the reflection he puts down
his revolver,
Careful and gentle like a new-born babe.
He rummages through his pockets,
And offers me a cigarette.
I take it as he lights us up,
His dead eyes reflecting the match light,
As war wages about us.

He speaks no English,
And I no German.
So we sit in peculiar calmness,

Under the whizzing bullets and bursting
shells,
And shake the mud from our hair,
And dust ourselves off,
And smoke,
Together.

# Your Country Needs You!

Your Country Needs You!
So says the country,
Whose spokesmen sing speeches,
Of kings and courage,
That stir men's hearts and lives.

Your Country Needs You!
So says the country,
Whose spokesmen wave their fists,
And threaten war to the warless,
Who strive for peace,
And life.

Your Country Needs You!
So says the country,
Whose spokesmen prattle,
Of the glorious conquest,
To the poor and impoverished,
Men of the masses.

Your Country Needs You!
So says my country,
Whose countrymen echo songs,
Of the Kings Shilling,
And work that feeds their children,

Who are too young to care for war,
Too young to matter to the country,
That by my rifle,
Has neither care nor need for them.

.

# White Feather

Sylvia presses a white feather into my hand,
And looks away,
In disgust.

I look at the white feather in my hand,
And look at her,
With forgiveness.

# What is Left?

What is left?
But ruined fields and broken men.

What is left?
But countless dead and dying.

What is left?
But scarred hearts and hate filled minds.

What is left?
But fleeting hope and wearied peace.

What is left?
But the promise of war.

# 11/11/1918

At the eleventh hour,
Of the eleventh day,
Of the eleventh month,
The guns stunned the world with silence.
An eerie quiet that stirred numbed souls,
And wetted men's eyes.
For the message could be heard in that
silence,
A message of peace out of war.
For the war was finally over.
Dead and buried with its dead,
Free to haunt the living,
At the eleventh hour,
Of the eleventh day,
Of the eleventh month,
Forevermore.

# The Cold

We huddle here,
Out in the cold.
Hands numb,
Feet dead,
Breath waltzing in the air.
Wind chills us,
Snapping at clothes,
Snatching at skin.
We shiver,
As night sleets seep aches into bones,
And sickness into heads.
Our constant tormentor –

*It'll be frosty tomorrow*,

So we huddle tighter together,
Out in the cold.

# Zep Down!

"Zep down!" call the spectators.
Eyes wide with frenzied terror,
As the blaze of orange devours,
And flaming jaws consume,
The silver that burns to ash.
Acrid smoke,
Blacker than the night,
Is belched across the sky,
Smothering the stars,
While people scream,
As the falling wreck,
Dives into their city,
Into their hearts,
Laying ruin to their lives.
"Zep Down!" cry the survivors.

# Scarborough Town

Our town of Scarborough town,
Is but a graveyard by the sea.
For the Hun have cast wide their nets,
And fished our boys from the water.
They came back to their mothers in pieces.
Burnt and disfigured and drowned.
Poor remains of the poor,
Who fight for another day,
That never comes.
For the days roll into one sorrowful wake,
Blighty's bluest blight,
That weeps in the veils of fog,
That roll off the sea,
To haunt us with their ghosts,
Here in our town,
Of Scarborough town.

# Recovering Jim

*We heard him.*

Out in that hell of shells and bullets and gas.
Not so much a screamer was our Jim.
But that day he screamed.
A whimper at first,
But as his blood drained from his wounds,
And his life watered the earth,
His dignity gave way to primitive wails,
And animalistic calls for survival.

*Officers told us that he was beyond help.*

We argued we could get him,
Save him from his plight,
And us from madness.
But we were told, "No"
"And that's an order private."
So we sat trying to block his shrieks and
screams from our thoughts.
But with each shrill shout,
His suffering was hammered into our skulls
like white hot nails,
Ringing terror into war wearied minds.

*When he died we cried out our relief.*

For we had lived and died with our Jim.
When the officers told us to go get him,
Few wanted the task.
If we could not reach him in life,
We had no right to reach him in death.
But we were told, "No"
"And that's an order private."
So we went over the top at sundown,
When the Hun settled in for the night,
And set about recovering Jim.

*He was not hard to find.*

For he had fallen a few feet from our trench,
But lay awkwardly in the mud.
Hands clasped around the hole in his
shoulder,
Where the sniper had got him good,
Leaking like uncorked claret.
But it was his eyes that got me the most.
Pale and wild and frightened,
Mad-like they burrowed into my soul,
Like the bullets that had burrowed into his
body.
Guilt gripped me that day,
And I've never been rid of it since.

*Sorry Jim.*

# Looking Back

Looking back I often wonder why.
But then I work myself into a state.
As frenzied as when I was there,
Dressed in my khaki with clean cold rifle in
hand.
Panic consumes me then,
As it always did.
My heart races,
And my throat closes over…

I can't breathe…

This world spins around me,
As echoes of another ring in my ears,
Those distant sounds of whiz bangers and
howitzers,
Against the rat-a-tat of gunfire,
And the screams of the living and dying –

But as history taps me on my left shoulder,
A solitary tear trails its way down my cheek.
An old tear from even older eyes - I come
back to my present then,
As my carer,
A Polish girl of twenty something,
Taps me on my right shoulder and asks me,
"What is wrong?"

"Nothing" I lie, "Just looking back."
"Well, no good comes from looking back,"
she smiles sweetly.

I sigh then.

For I know that more than most.

# Broken

The Great War broke many men and many
more boys.
It took their bodies and maimed them,
And tortured their tormented souls.
It sowed seeds of madness in minds,
And killed their hope of normality.
For war is far from normal.
And those who feel its merciless touch,
Are far from normal by their end.
For they are the countless souls,
Nameless save for their common name.

Broken.

# Remembrance

Every year we are told to remember,
And pay them our respects,
By the sound of Big Ben,
Whose eleven morning chimes,
Mark the occasion of remembrance.
And so for two minutes,
We stand in dignified silence,

And think about EastEnders…

Or what to have for dinner…

*BOGOF on pasta sauce,*
*Yeah - that'll do for tea.*

Tweets and pokes,

Tags and shameless screens,

Nothing at all…

But who can blame us?
For we cannot remember what we have
never witnessed.
Nor can we imagine the hells of The Great
War,
Or wars ever since,

In those one hundred and twenty passing
seconds,
Of standing silence,
In the still shadows of cenotaphs.

For the occasion of remembrance,
Is one of quiet ignorance.

# White Cliffs

Through the fog of sea and the fug of war,
We see them then.
The white cliffs.
They stand a wall of defiance.
A chalk glacier rising from the grey drab of
the channel pass.
Imperious they salute us.
A reminder of hope and home,
That thaws our hearts ablaze with passion,
As waterfalls flow with sorrowful tears.
The numbness leaves our spirits then.
An aching pain rushes over us.
Our relief is tainted with remorse,
And bitter regret.
But we see them,
Those white cliffs,
And our spirit rises,
Like the waves that carry us from hell.
For they stand.

As we stand.

# Guns at Dawn

When the morning rises in the east,
As dew clings to the living dead.

When birds sing out their early call,
As frosts blanket the fallen.

When men stir from fevered slumber,
As the air wafts with sickly scents.

When sentries exchange their duty,
As duty binds the dutiful.

When the world wakes,
As the world sleeps.

When the ignorant ignore,
As the ignored take notice.

Manufactured thunder, a deafening din,
Sound the guns at dawn.

# On Leave

I'm on leave.

But I'm never on leave.

Not really,

Not truly.

I can sample the delights of the ignorant,
Indulge in their pleasures of the flesh.
Brothels and food and spirits,
Can sway my senses,
And distract my mind.
But I cannot ignore the front.
Not when I'm awake,
Nor when I'm asleep.


I'm on leave.

But I'm never on leave.

Not really,

Not truly.

I can visit my family,

Strange strangers at home,
Who knew me once when I was a boy,
When I was their boy.
But I'm nobody now,
For I am on leave of my body and mind.
I'm always on leave me,

Yes really,

Yes truly.

For I cannot ignore the front.
Not when I'm awake,
Nor when I'm asleep.

# Letters

Letters pass between two fronts steeped in
their stagnation.
They fly like paper birds,
Carrying sweet messages of love and hope,
That pass before strangers who censor their
truth away.
Adding to that great lie of the effort,
That most contemptable of lies,
That send boys meekly to their end.
The lie of glory,
Deluded until its end –
But still the letters do fly,
A comfort to their sanity,
That keep the mundane of food parcels and
socks,
And talk of Mrs. Green at number four,
A part of their every day,
despite the worry of another day.
And loved ones echo from envelopes,
Opened on each other's doorstep.
For a front door in Sunderland,
And the frontline of the Somme,
Are two of the same;
Two fronts steeped in stagnant war,
Breached only by the passing of letters.

# Birdsong

When we few packed up and made for
home,
And left our shame in ditches,
And pieces of ourselves in fields,
Silence descended.
And the land drank of rain,
That washed the soil of blood,
And healed it with greenest shoots,
As life returned to that hell.

Poppies bloomed in sunlight,
As fresh grass shivered in spring breezes,
And insect melodies rejoiced in nature's
splendour.

Then came the birds,
Who returned to their kingdom,
And nestled in trees and bushes,
That blossomed as fields bloomed in peace.

They sang then,
Those sweet birds,
Of blue tits, and sparrows, and finches,
Sweet songs at dawn,
Filling the skies with chirps and tweets –
A chorus of life.

For miles they trumpeted their triumph over
death,
That had driven them away those dark years.
A jubilant sound,
A most majestic sound,
Calm and peaceful.
For nothing is as beautiful,
Nor as healing,
As birdsong.

# Silence

As I sit here,

Locked in a room,

With four walls,

A ceiling,

And a door,

I feel trapped.

Not because I despise rooms,
But because since the war,
Where the walls were mud,
Ceilings were ever skyward,
And doors were but a figment of home,
I have had to eat, sleep and exist,
With the noise of war.

But now that I am away from all that,
There is only silence,
And I'm its prisoner.

Silence.

That vast emptiness assaults my ears,

And lays siege to my mind.
It follows me in thought and being.
A sinister stillness saturating war sore
senses.
A threatening,
And foreboding vacuum,
That fills my heart with a dread,
I never encountered on the front.

For I welcomed the front and its distracting
noise,
Of almighty gunfire,
Of the screaming injured and insane,
Of the wailing shells and the whimpers of
the dying.
That has been the instrumental din of my
being.
But now that such disturbance has ceased,
The silence has focussed my mind,
On things I would rather forget.

Some say that silence is deafening,
I say silence is a killer.
An assassin in the shadows of scenes I've
witnessed.
Slow and steady it stalks and stirs me with
sinister caress,
From my waking sleep.
And when I awake,

I will sleep then.

In silence.

# Blighty

Few here remember that far away land,
Whose trees whisper in summer breezes,
And streams bubble and babble,
Under the north star.
That brightest of stars,
That glistens and glimmers in watchful
peace,
Over that faraway land,
Of Blighty.

Few here remember that faraway land,
Whose quaint villages bustle in quiet
ignorance,
Rushing through each day with distracted
minds,
That long to wake from war,
That never-ending war,
So that their loved ones might return,
To that faraway land,
Of Blighty.

Few here remember that faraway land,
That distant land of hearth and home,
Of health and happiness.
A place we few left for soldiering.
A land of love and a land of hope,
That has long since dimmed,

For few here remember,
That faraway land,
Of Blighty.

# Suits and Boots

As boots march their standstill march,
Through fire and mud and water.
Suits converge on matters,
And the fools play God.

Their games are crafty,
Craftily crafted by creatures robed in starchy
shirts,
While boys in lice clad clobber dirty their
boots on the board,
Booted pawns of the suited.

When peace is declared through suited
mouths,
And the game is over,
Some boots limp home,
While others rot.
For boots lose more than others,
And suits lose less than most.

# Munitionettes

Munitionettes are a strange folk,
With their crowns of wild green,
Glowing skin,
Eyes golden.
They busy away all day all night,
Fingers scratched sore to bony twigs,
That work hastily on shells and bullets,

To kill,

Those sons and husbands and brothers,
Uncles and friends of the Hun,

And protect,

Their sons and husbands and brothers,
Their uncles and friends from old Fritzie.

For Tommies are armed by canaries,
Who sing sweet songs,
Those mothers and wives,
Sisters and aunties,
Who will their men safety,
With wishes as fleeting as the wind,
But who manufacture their danger.
Equipping their loves with loveless love.
A strange folk,

Those Munitionettes.

# Widows

Widows wail on doorsteps,
When men bring death to their hearts.
Their dreamy hope of lovers return,
Shatters like the shells that took them,
And poured grief into their souls,
As tears overflow,
Forevermore.

Prisoners to the void,
That consumes their being,
With aches and unseen pain.
An invisible blight of their future,
That lies dim and beyond sight.

Time wheels overhead,
As fogs roll into minds,
Like veils that drape,
In tormented sorrow,
Those widows who wail on doorsteps,
When men bring death to their hearts.

# Fever

Fever grips the world.
Infecting minds and plaguing bodies,
With all the contagions of war.

Boys kill in bloodlusts,
Excused with lies of glory,
By men behind their desks.

Statesmen peddle to their state,
That sways in fevered rhythm,
To their sick songs of contest.

Mothers wave sons to their death,
While fathers watch with blinded pride,
And mates cheer each other on to hell.

For those brave fools will come to flirt each
day,
With their end that looms over them,
Their silent spectre,

Murder.

That flies over this earth on black wings of
ravens,
Whose blinking eyes witness the slaughter,
And caw their decadent delight as,

Fever grips the world.
Infecting minds and plaguing bodies,
With all the contagions of war.

# Medals

Each shining medal that glimmers glorious
on ribbons,
Is but a hollow tribute to what they went
through.
Empty reminders,
Token gestures,
Sad symbols of empathy,
By innocents who know not what it was
like,
To nestle in muddy holes and trenches,
And witness living hells that torment,
When battles have ended and fields heal and
faces fade.

*How could they know?*

When pinning their tin disks,
Of war's incense of rotting flesh,
While wading through the death of the front.
Or of the wailing pleas for mercy,
By those strung up on the wire,
Or blown to bits over the top.

*How could they know?*

Of the countless dead. The dying,
Of the brotherly bonds between broken men,

Who returned to broken homes that shunned
them,
When they needed home the most.

For this deceit cannot be believed,
That each shining medal,
That glimmers gloriously on ribbons,
Is a worthy testament to the brave.
For medals are but an empty symbol;
Cold and lifeless,
Metal dangling from synthetic fabrics,
As dead as the souls who went through it,
For their descendants,
For us,
That century ago.

# Mrs. Campbell

Mrs. Campbell was never the same the day
her Robert left her.
She had known about his mistress,
But had chosen to ignore,
And plead her ignorance,
To herself.

There were times she pretended all was well,
But she knew her Robert.
She knew he would succumb to her
seductions.
Like a bee tempted by the pollen of flowers,
He would satisfy his urges,
Lose his control,
And she would lose him then.
But what chance did she have?
For his mistress was a rush of excitement,
A sordid thrill of newness. Journeys.
Adventure.
While his doting Doris was a dour reminder
of the sedentary,
Of the mundane. Drudgery. Life's many
disappointments.
She could sense that truth within him.
A fleeting glance,
An awkward pause,
Told her all she needed to know.

A thousand words spoken without a single
word escaping his lips.

If it wasn't for her fear of losing him,
Of living without her Robert,
She knew he would have gone to her sooner.
But even then she knew it was only a matter
of time,
For time corrupts,
And when the time came,
And it did,
Grief got her and never let her go.

He told her in the kitchen that day,
Kitbag packed and ready.
She begged and pleaded and promised him
the world,
But it wasn't enough.
She knew that.
She had always known that…

And so she slouched on the kitchen floor,
Head resting on the cold iron stove,
Heart crushed in the iron grip of her misery,
Spirit broken by his iron will,
As he went to her then,
His mistress.


War.

# Tanks and Tears

And tears roll down men's cheeks,
As tanks roll down the hill.

Great beasts bolting to their front,
In slow and steady inches.

Churning up earth and stomach,
As they loom up ahead.

Steel plated devils,
That haunt men in their waking dreams.

Stopping hearts in heaving chests,
As they bury living souls in the mud.

They scour the field for their enemies,
Like a wingless vulture surveying its prey.

Men targeting men,
Within war's metallic belly.

Before firing its bullets and shells,
As their tank rolls down the hill,

And tears roll down their cheeks.

# For Whom the Bell Tolls

Men marched to hell and back,
Boys robbed of youth.
Widows and their broken hearts,
Conchies and their truth.

Nurses and their bedside grief,
Conscripts and their say.
Officers who censored truth,
The price all men must pay.

Shell-shocked and their silent wake,
Grieving family ties.
Broken men ignored by most,
The most deceived by lies.

Sons buried in Flanders mud,
Brothers bound in battle.
Survivors maimed and ignored,
Treated worse than cattle.

Those whose future never passed,
Poor dispirited souls.
Defeated victors of the last,
For whom the bell tolls.

# Desertion

My rifle drops.
Artillery colliding.
Crashing.
Cavorting.
Ammunition crackling.
Popping.
Bursting like seeds.
My head spins and sways,
This way and that.
This world makes no sense anymore.
Adrenaline.
Frightened.
Rush.

Boots squelch in mud,
That desperate jailer.
Whistles squeal the advance,
Men scream out their terror,
Brave faced as they climb ladders,
Marching past,
To futures end.

Their wild eyes catch mine.
Questioning.
Judging.
I can't breathe. I need air.

I gasp and collide with brothers,
And push them away,
As the earth steals my boots.
Hungry for scraps,
It will not let me go…

I stumble,
And crawl,
And rid myself of it then.

And lay down my duty,
And take up my freedom,
Of desertion.

# The Hun

The beady eyed and sneering smile,
Weak furrow browed cowards,
That mock and jeer from the other side,
With their foreign tongues.
The Hun.
Who laugh at our expense.
Those honourless gentlemen,
A caste of monsters.
Strange faced abominations,
That poke and prod and taunt,
And flex with witless words.
They drive this world to its depravity.
Why could they not refrain,
And exchange pleasantries of peace?

Why?

But then I remember.
I remember my truth,
And not the truth we have swallowed.
For there is no Hun.
There never was.
I've been to see them,
Out there on the other side,
And all I saw,
Was myself,
Blinking back at me.

# Brothers

Those brothers,
Who were strangers,
Bound by blood and arms.

Those brothers,
Who were strangers,
Seduced by bugle charms.

Those brothers,
Who were strangers,
Broken by war alarms.

Those brothers,
Who were strangers,
Exiled from town and farms.

Those brothers,
Who were strangers,
Tormented by gnawing qualms.

Those brothers,
Who were strangers,
Abandoned to prayers and psalms.

Those brothers,
Who were strangers,
Bound in blood and arms.

# Leapfrogging

Laughter.
Oh the hilarity!
The cobbles echo our excitement.
A fools march.
Like lemmings lurching to the edge.
Leapfrogging hysterical,
Embracing happy abandon.

Laughter.
Oh the hilarity!
As we rush to the front.
Pals fevered with delusions,
Believing in the great illusion.
That sounds the applause,
Of bystander choruses.

Laughter.
Oh the hilarity!
As sickening giggles escape corpse's
mouths.
A maddening sound,
Leapfrogging to hell.
Few hear the guns,
That call out our end.
Who'll be laughing then?

# The Rush

A fire burns through the ache,
And eats away the pain.
Its heat loosens dead limbs,
As excitement stirs the spirit,
That sleeps in the dark of the soul,
Shying from the terror.

The guns call to fear,
That stokes the fire,
That burns through the ache,
And eats away the pain.
A heat most frightening.
Warmly welcomed.
A frenzied front that calls the mind,
And body,
To take up arms and indulge in the rush.

# War Horses

Hear the whinnying horses,
Baptised in the chaos of war.

Know that they bleed with their masters,
As they lie sprawled on the battlefield floor.

Their beauty marked by conflict,
Their trust betrayed by man.

Oh hear the whinnying horses,
That cry in the chaos of war.

Know that they sink in the mud pits,
And drown on the battlefield floor.

Their bodies shot and lame,
Their spirits drowned in pain.

Oh hear the whinnying horses,
That die in the chaos of war.

# Bound

Animals shackled to man,
By invisible bonds that bind,
As war calls on the animal.
Chickens and cows ensnared to the effort,
As sheep flock to their masters.
Horses broken by lead ropes,
That break the stallion to human will.
Pigeons and canaries sing songs,
Laments for the wild.
Dogs and cats kept as pets,
Long to go inside.
As do the men,
Who are shackled to animals,
By invisible bonds that tie,
A most tragic meeting of beasts,
Like slaughtered slaves to the slaughtered,
Bound to a common abattoir.

# Flight

Up here man can fly on wooden wings,
And indulge his senses in the flight.
But aside from the grandeur of distance,
And its dazzling spectacle of horizons end,
Therein lies the ugly majesty of war.

That foul business that rolls before the
heavens,
Carpeting the land with fields of blood,
And bones.
The winds whisper of agony,
As death throes carry to the sky,
And sickening aromas hint of a grounded
hell.

But up here man can fly on wooden wings,
And indulge his senses in the flight.
If only they could see what we few see,
Up here in the kingdom of birds and clouds.
Then perhaps that would be the end of it.
And mankind might soar,
Once again.

# Sweethearts

She waits for me in Blighty,
Behind a door closed off to the front.
Hoping that I might survive,
The terror of old Fritzie's hunt.

She holds the key to my being,
Without her I'm a stranger to myself.
For she is my love, my life, my soulmate,
Who prays for my safekeeping and health.

For we are each other's sweethearts,
And our love will outlast this war.
And if death should bother to take us,
We'll remain sweethearts forevermore.

# Clouds

From their mud pits and trenches,
Soldiers peer into the heavens,
And drift like the clouds that drift overhead.
They forget about the grind of war,
And imagine floating like those clouds,

Blown by foreign headwinds,

To faraway places…

To forests and vast open plains,
Pine blanketed mountains and roaring
crystal falls,
Windswept deserts and shimmering barren
glaciers,
Bubbling rivers and tide lapped shores,
Bustling towns and manic frenzied cities…

Home.

And in that moment,
Tears wash the stinging sadness from
worried eyes,
As they remember,
The sun,
breaks through the sky then,
Offering the hopeless hope,

As clouds drift from their minds.

# Passchendaele

That field of mindless slaughter,
That cursed the youthful living,
As rains swept over the heads,
Of killers made too giving.

Passchendaele they called it,
That senseless battle of waste.
Where boys rushed in their thousands,
And fell dying in their haste.

Countless shells were fired,
As millions marched maimed.
But few could dissuade the generals,
Who pushed on unashamed.

Both sides sank in stalemate,
As soldiers began to tire,
Of stinking water and rotting meat.
Exposed to weather and fire.

Those heroes died in horrors,
That few can now believe.
Drowned in swamps of mud and men,
That battle longed to grieve.

Those who survived that dale,
And its passions of fear and murder,

Left marked by the sickening schemes,
Of butcher Haig the herder.

Some rest beneath stones now,
White rows of the forgotten,
While others lie in earthy crypts,
Among worms and roots most rotten.

But they still lie there those fallen,
In that field of mindless slaughter,
To remind the living of their hell,
Of war and soiled water.

Passchendaele they called it,
That senseless battle of waste.
Where boys rushed in their thousands,
And fell dying in their haste.

# Rebirth

Out of fire and water,
I rise from the filth and dirt,
And lay down my fear.
I am free now save for the shackles of war,
That chain me to its spectacle,
And gift me perspective.
For now I am one of a few,
Who has awoken to mortality,
And that prescient delusion,
That life is forever,
And death is an exile.

Out of this nightmare,
I know now that life is fleeting,
And death is a companion, who whispers,
Every second, of every day,
Every breath,
Every passing heartbeat – precious.

I entered the front an excitable boy,
And witnessed his death.
But now I am reborn of fire and water and
mud and dirt – A rebirth of war,
So that I might live again until my end,
When I will fade into memory,
Like so many before me,
Knowing that I knew death,

And had lived.

# New Arrivals

They arrive dressed for war,
But their hearts are not in it.
For they have yet to see,
And their eyes are as green as their khaki.

They laugh and joke and whistle,
Until they hear the whistles,
That stirs them from themselves,
As they are forced wide awake.

Their faces drop then,
As they face the desolation.
And witness the shells,
And meet the maimed who embraced them.

They wretch at the stench of latrines,
And vomit at the aromas of the dying.
Their eyes grow wet with tears,
Though all deny they're crying.

They watch on dazed as soldiers scream for order,
In the chaos that consumes them.
Bullets zing over heads – that causes them to flinch,
While some duck like children before old Fritzies guns.

One of them messes himself then,
As a shell lands on our side.
They thought they knew what war is,
But they know not what awaits them,

In their trench nor their mind.

# Boys to Men

They were sent away as boys,
Lambs led to slaughter.
Many did not make it,
And many more were changed,
In ways that few could understand.
For they saw things that could not be
unseen,
And such sights lingered,
So that when they returned,
They knew not home or themselves.

The war had altered them.

From boys to men who were heroes and
survivors,
Victims – broken husks,
Who carried dark secrets of the front,
To the dark of their graves,
Like ghosts vowed to silence.
For these men the war never ended,
Not really,
Not truly.
It was death in the end that caught up with
them,
And ended it.

# The Storm

A storm brews overhead,
And the fronts squabble below.
Black clouds cast foreboding shadows
across the chaos.
As gusts of wind snatch at soldiers with
hidden claws.
Lightning dazzles in the distance,
A fork of bright destruction,
Piercing from the heavens,
That shower minds with falsehoods and lies.
The thunderous din of battle,
Drowns the rolling thunder,
That hails the presence of fitful fears,
As men cower in their own mortality.

The storm lives and breathes,
As the men below live and die,
And souls take the mortal pass,
Bodies left behind to shrivel and fade.
At times sunlight breaks through the dark,
But such light flickers as it falls on the
fallen,
Whose war is a storm of its own.
A maelstrom of perfected chaos,
Destroying that which was pure,
Corrupting that which was innocent,
Ageing that which was young.

While the storm overhead may calm,
Their storm,
That frightening tempest of life,
Rages with the spirit of all who live to see
such times,
From their first breath,
To their last.

# Family Ties

Family is what helped them,
Those brothers and fathers and sons.
Ties are what got them through it,
As they stared down German guns.

Family is what helped them,
As they marched to hell for death.
Ties are what got them through it,
As they took their final breath.

Family is what helped them,
While they huddled in rain.
Ties are what got them through it,
When the wounded went insane.

Family is what helped them,
When their pals went over the top.
Ties are what got them through it,
When the bullets failed to stop.

Family is what helped them,
When they witnessed the senseless
slaughter.
Ties are what got them through it,
As they waged war in mud and water.

Family is what helped them,

When disease and sickness infected.
Ties are what got them through it,
Those solders the war affected.

# Games

War games are played on Flanders Fields,
That are sowed with crops of death.
Men are like seeds whose lives are laid
down,
For the players to tend and harvest in their
sick schemes,
And abuse in selfish strategies,
As they play out their games of chance,
Their games of loss,
A game for players,
The game of war.
That old game.
That winless game.
Where all must lose,
And play for survival,
Until the players grow weary,
Or tired,
Or bored,
And decide to play a new game.

And so starts another war.

# Life

Life is precious – I know that now.
When you see your friends go,
And their faces fade from your mind,
That is when it gets to you.
That is when you understand.

As war wages about you,
You recognise the frail truth,
That is locked in every passing breath,
In every fleeting heartbeat,
Every passing moment,
Every instant.

Bullets usually take life,
But life can end in other ways,
Beyond the mechanics of war.
Sickness can do it,
At home as much as at the front.
And a dodgy ticker need not be in France to
conk out on you.
An act of maddening stupidity can take life
on both sides of the channel,
Of that we can all agree.

Deep down you know this to be true,
But distractions distract,
And hearts yearn to be distracted.

But death accompanies us regardless.
A constant reminder that life is precious – I
know that now.

For we who fight in this war,
Know that more than most.

# Dig

Surrounded on three sides by the enemy,
We dig into the soil of Ypres,
And pray for a swift victory.

Our guns hammer this foreign land,
And leave its countrymen with destruction,
The like of which we have never seen.

For miles across the salient,
Villages and towns smoke and crumble.
Devastated ruins that cast broken shadows

across mud churned fields that poison rivers,
That bleed from broken banks,
And lick broken roots of decaying trees.

What have we done?
No bird sings here.
Life has left this place.

We hunker down in waste,
As this unending tempest wreaks its
destruction,
Killing this Eden until the end.

The enemy responds in kind,
And gifts us shells and bullets,

Early Christmas presents wrapped in
sickness and death.

Though there is nothing festive about this
world,
Ruined by passionate minds plagued with
madness,
And fear.

But we have come too far to turn back now.
So surrounded on three sides by the enemy,
We dig into the soil of Ypres.

And pray.

# Boredom

Between the orders to push,
Like a woman forcing a breach,
We sit huddled among the mud,
And sit amongst the boredom.

It's fine when the rush of action,
Numbs the mind with distraction,
Pouring excitement into wearied limbs,
As we go forth to tackle the Bosch.

But when we sit idle,
And let our minds wander,
The boredom soon gets us,
And torments us like the cold.

Days and nights roll together,
Into a life age of routine,
Broken save for a snipers dance,
Or a trip to the stinking latrine.

Yes you can clean your rifle,
But monotony reminds you of hell,
That time of foolish excitement,
When me and my pals laughed to the front.
But when they fell at the Somme,
I lost my laughter and locked my smile
away.

So as battles are won or lost,
We sit amongst the mud,
And sit among the boredom,
And fear it,

For it leads minds to darker places,
Than the one we now call home.

# Survive

The instinct is there,
Rushing to every limb,
With every heartbeat,
I clamber from the trench then.
And pray that I survive.

My pals fall beside me,
Some trip on wire,
Others choke on bullets.
But I keep stumbling forward.
And pray that I survive.

The instinct is still there,
Though my mind clouds over,
As I peer through the smoke and mist,
And walk forwards,
And pray that I survive.

Shells arrive then,
And greet us with towers of earth,
As more men fall about me.
I walk over them in bits.
And pray that I survive.

Men scream and roar for death.
The living and the dying.
I fire rounds aimlessly into the chaos,

And jab my bayonet out in front,
And pray that I survive.

Shrapnel then greets me,
My neck a sticky mess,
War's sickest love bite,
As I fall with the rest.

And I pray that I survive.

# Wounded

A crescent of light dawns before me,
A flood of cascading day.
I'm alive.
My neck is wrapped,
Pain lingers but the shrapnel's sharp
embrace,
Has left a stinging head as a parting gift.

A nurse props up my starch stiff pillow,
A welcome change from coarse damp sand
bags.
Her sweet face,
Soothing radiance with almond eyes of
amber,
And that smile. So warm. Distracts me from
myself.
A brief respite from shells and souls.

I peer into those honeyed gemstones,
And in their gloss and shine I see a broken
man.
Lying with a face as pale as the white sheets,
That lie heavy across his rattling chest,
Loose drapes hanging from a wilting
skeleton.
His lips cracked and off colour,
Neck bulging with bandages,

Stained and soiled.
A look in his lost eyes…

"wounded," a voice echoes from within.

But I'm not worried about such flesh
wounds.
For like the man that fades in those almond
mirrors,
I worry for the wounds that can't be seen,
That can't be put to bed,
That can't be bandaged.
I worry for the hidden,
The shrapnel of memories.
That snag,
And tear,
And rip,
Each and every second of every cursed day,
Until their wounds grow old and infected,
And my mind gives out.

Let's hope I'm asleep before then.

# Shot at Dawn

They were led out,
Those deserters and madmen and boys.
And told to stand by that wall,
That everyone fears,
And few ever see.

They were ordered to remain silent,
Though they rarely spoke.
For a skeletal hand rests on them,
Brushing hair from frightened faces,
Rubbing cold into backs,
Offering a final squeeze of a shoulder.

Tears well in their empty eyes,
And flee like those who abandoned them to
such fate.
Those poor souls were human once.
Pals sat huddled with the riflemen.
But now they are pitied as lame animals.
And treated just the same.

The order comes swift and hard,
When loaded guns steady aim.
Until a chorus of pulled triggers,
Send bullets into skulls,
As those deserters and madmen and boys,
Are shot at dawn,

In the name of glory.

In the name of honour.

In the name of King.

In the name of country.

Names that died that day,

And every following day,

When brave men were plucked from hell,
And shot for the sport of deserters and
madmen and boys.

# Armed Pacifist

I am an armed pacifist.
A hypocrite – yes I know.
A figure of broken values,
Who swapped peace for rounds of ammo.

But please do not judge me,
For a conscript has no choice.
And if I had taken their feather,
I'd forever have lost my voice.

But I do not worry,
For I'll not pull the trigger.
And kill in the name of futile wars,
Despite the souls who snigger.

I am an armed pacifist,
But a pacifist nonetheless.
And I will not arm my weapons,
Or have a hand in this their madness.

This will undoubtedly mean court martial.
Of that we can both be sure.
But in my choice of peaceful means,
I hope you'll find the cure.

For underneath the Khaki,
We are still children of man.

Whose hearts and minds still yearn for
peace,
That'll end this war's sick plan.

I am an armed pacifist,
And I'll forever hold out for peace.
So while you wage war about me,
I pray your war will cease.

For I will not kill another,
For the sake of a killing game.
Why should I murder you, brother.
Have we all lost our shame?

# Homeless

Before my return home I was made
homeless.
And when I returned neighbours looked
away,
As family turned their backs.

*I was their sitting shame.*

A hero save for the missing legs,
That lie in that foreign meadow.
They looked at me with pity at first,
Love lost eyes fading at the crippled
stranger.

*They had learnt to forget.*

And told me it was best that I leave.
So I left my home as I did those few years
before,
And now sit shivering again in winter frosts.
Pitied by disgusted strangers.

*My family have spread falsehoods of my
death.*

So I am homeless and alone here in a
country of appearances,

For my true home is back in the trenches,
Chancing with life,
Dicing with death.

*I owe my legs to the curse of that war's*
*reaper.*

Who stole them in that mine blast,
And left me a humbled man.
Lonely save for the ghostly memories,
Of a different life,
From the one I'm now living.

*For now I am homeless.*

# At Sea

We're all at sea as battleships ride the crests,
And fire wicked bullets and torpedoes,
That explode like storms of flame that lick,
Our broken hull.
Belching blackest smog that smothers all
light,
A confusing curtain of shadow.

*We can't escape. We can't get out.*

The hull screeches.
A screeching, screaming, shrieking sound of
scraping metal.
That jitters the poor boys of Jutland.

Bullets as big as fingers rat-a-tat from across
the rabid waves,
And bury into hulls of metal and bone.
Men scream then,
Louder than any screaming metal.

*We can't escape. We can't get out.*

We're all at sea as water fills our belly,
Drowning men already drowned in destiny.
We clamber through the fiery curtain,
Choking on smoke hot and stinging,

That singes hair and blisters skin.
Diesel burning nostrils,
As battleships play out their tragic dance on
the abyss.

*We can't escape. We can't get out.*

The lifeboats have abandoned us,
As empty as our hope that we may stay
afloat.
Survive.
Water flows over the top deck then,
To claim us.
Our stomachs lurch unsteady as we sink into
salty froths.
Steady at first,

and then,

Drowned.

# Ghosts

I settle in for the night,
And see the ghosts of my present,
Make their cursed march to die and die
again.
Their translucent bodies glisten as if clothed
in moonlit dew.
They glow eerily as they stumble over the
top.
Most don't know that I'm watching,
But Percy does.
Percy always takes the time to look back,
And over his silvery shoulder our eyes meet.
A shared moment between the dead.

He turns from me then and retraces his
steps,
Out across that pitted and cratered hell.
But my mind replays his last steps long after
he has gone.
All of their last steps.
Ivor, Stan, Cecil, Wilfred –
They haunt my waking thoughts,
And visit me in my dreams.

*Always silent.*
*Always sombre.*
*Always sad.*

For they are the fallen who watch over the
fallen.
Ghostly spectacles doomed to restless sleep,
Who torment those they left in their wake,
And remind me of that fact.

So I settle in for the night,
And make peace with the ghosts of my
present,
And prepare to make my cursed march,
Across their graveyard,

Of no man's land.

# Locked Up

Locked up for caring.
Locked up for trying.
Locked up for daring.
Locked up for crying.

Locked up for madness,
By madmen young and old.
Locked up for showing cowardice,
By the herded who always fold.

Locked up for being human.
Locked up for being me.
Locked up for the sake of unions,
In whose wars I disagree.

Locked up for saying no.
Locked up for choosing life.
Locked up because I know,
This Great War's greater strife.

Locked up because I cared,
Locked up because I tried.
Locked up because I dared,
To save the men who died.

# Scarred

Underneath the flesh wounds,
That faded into silvery lines,
Deep within the dark that no light can
breach,
A place within all of us.
A vast and open place.
As big and as small as can be imagined,
Empty and filled,
A sanctuary where suppressed wounds
fester.
Lingering. Tormenting. Haunting,
The veterans of that war,
Who now lie scattered in open fields,
Or laid to rest – God bless them.
Most went to the grave distressed,
Chaperoned by grief and pain.
Alone.
Memories snagging like the wire.
Echoing dark times in that darkest of places,
Distracted until they re-joined their brothers,
When they went over the top,
One final time.

# Alone

I lie here alone save for the stars that twinkle
from heaven.
I look to them up there in the freezing black.
But they look on from an unreachable
kingdom.
Their cold light a distant offering of faded
hope.

*I know that I will die out here.*

My legs have grown numb now,
And my blood leaks into the mud,
That does not drink of it,
No doubt it has had its fill of blood these
days.
Part of me wishes that it will take me
instead,
And swallow me down into its dank depths,
So that I may drown in the land that I lie on.
For I will no longer be alone then.
I'll be in the company of thousands out here.
I would lie among them and join their
watch,
As others come stumbling over the top,
And march to battle to join us.

*I hope my teeth don't chatter too loudly.*

For I might disturb the souls who stalk this
hell,
And send for my sniper.
But then I remember,
I'm alone.

Memories come rushing to me,
Unstoppable as rivers,
But they bring me no comfort.
For the cold has robbed me of their warmth.
Family and friends haunt me,
And dance in the dark,
Of my end.
Their cheerful faces sting my heart,
As tears sting my eyes,
And freeze upon my pale cheek,
Like tiny chips of diamond,
That glisten like those faraway stars –

*I shall die out here tonight.*

Alone.

# Hold the Line!

Hold the line! Hold the line!
We shout and shoot.
Struggle and stab.
Snatching at life.


Smoke and fog hide them.
The Hun. Old Fritzy. Boys.
Who rush at us,
In fitful rage.


Die linie halten! Die linie halten!
We shout and shoot.
Struggling to stab,
Struggling to live.

Smoke and fog hide us,
As we rush them,
Those English boys who defend,
In fitful rage.


Hold the line! Hold the line!
We shout like frenzied madmen,
But they come at us madder still.

Not even death can stop them. Too close.
Too near.


They shoot at us. Blank range.
And punch and kick when barrels are empty.
Hysterical with war sickness,
Broken they break us.


Die linie halten! Die linie halten!
They shriek now as we arrive with bullets,
And knives, And fists.
We get in closer than a mother's embrace,
And gift them a merciful end.


Some run into the mists then,
Made mad with shock.
While others lie dying,
And turn to strangers.


Hold the line! Hold the line!
The reserves have come too late.
The Germans have already got us,
But we're ordered to our deaths.


Most of us have fallen,
While others have lost themselves,

In the mists of war and mind.
But we few join the others standing.

Die linie halten! Die linie halten!
More of the poor souls come falling,
And shoot and stab,
With wild eyes. Fatigued hearts.

But one of them throws down his weapon,
Broken by the effort.
He argues sense within chaos,
As we push them back to their Blighty.

Hold the line! Hold the line!
I refuse and surrender my rifle.
I'm no soldier and this is not soldiering.
"This is honourless work sir – murder."

The murderer points at me then.
Revolver as black as his heart,
Blows a cold kiss into my skull,
That rings with, "Hold the line!"

# Memories

Memories haunt and memories linger.
I've kept them locked up all these years,
But in me they've found a prisoner.
I can never escape the trench I'm in,
I can never again breathe free air.
The scenes I have witnessed follow my
waking steps,
And the ghosts of the fallen frequent my
dreams,
So that they become nightmares as
frightening as Flanders.
I remember but long to forget.
But memories haunt and memories linger.
I've kept them locked up all these years,
But in me they've found their prisoner.

# In Memoriam

We thank you with soundless words,
That echo in clouded minds.

We honour you with beating hearts,
And forsaken breath.

We salute you in elevens,
And forget with passing years.

You fade with generations,
Pale faced shapes.

You are titled and bold,
Book covers fading in time.

You are feint words on shelves,
Exposed to cuts and backs.

You are spoken in memoriam,
Found in November speeches.

You are pinned to lapels,
Thrown in bins on the 12th.

We remember you with wreaths,
That wither when we leave.

As we drop silver into pots,
To gift ourselves reprieve.

# Changed

War changed them all, you know.

It changed them.

Yes it did.

Boys changed into broken men,
In fields that changed their home.
Mothers changed as they mothered grief,
And fathers changed their pride.
Siblings changed and lived alone.
Daddy changed into a ghost.
Wives changed into widows,
While sons changed into shells.
And friends changed into memories,
That haunted with the tolling of bells.

War changed them all, you know.

It changed them.

Yes it did.

# Lost and Found

I was lost out on the grim front.
Soul shocked from my senses,
So that it wandered empty in that maze,
As I lost myself to the war.

Again. Again. Again.

It took me with its wrath,
And stole my courage,
And showed me sick scenes that cast
hideous shadows across my mind.
My waking nightmare,
That darkened my sleep.
It frightened me from myself,
And left my life abandoned as a tomb.
Vacant, save for routines that carried me on,
and up,
and over the top,
where I wandered that day across no man's
land.

In body and spirit I meandered through hell,
Whose wicked gates were open,
Flooding that field,
With all manner of evil.

Time slowed there to lengthen the agony of
the men who fell in their thousands.
The land squelched with red that day,
And the air reeked with death.
But as shells and grenades and bullets
drowned the dying,
A fleeting moment stirred something deep
within.

Ears ringing, heart thumping, lungs burning
with smoke and phlegm.

I could feel again.

The numbness fell from me. A thawing
glacier.

A shame I took a bullet that day,

Lost as I was found.

# Horizon

Every day we sat in our trench and looked to
our horizon,
And knew that when the sun set on that
bleak day,
It would rise again on another,
And perhaps that would be the day that the
war finally ended.
And we who remained could pack up our
things and go back home –
*But,*
The days passed into one,
And the war carried on.
For our hope of the war's end,
Was as distant as the furthest point on that
horizon,
Our horizon.
Feint and remote and beyond our reach.

# Winter

When winter blizzards fell,
We fell from the cold that gnawed at our limbs,
And nibbled at the sore skin of our wearied bodies.
Snow seeped freezing damp into bones,
Stinging souls and teasing fatigued minds.
Winter is more frightening than war,
For she is cunning and careless.
She has no preference for victims.
English. German. Old. Young. Black. White –
It mattered not out there on that front.
On the edge of all that is right and sane,
For they all dropped to their knees before her,
And shivered to their graves in her presence.

So many brave men and courageous boys,
Survivors of unspeakable terrors,
Succumbed too easily to her cold embrace.
Weak as new born babes.

The few who avoided this fate,
Did so in the heat of battle.
For she could not touch them there,

Where their hearts and minds pulsed with
blood,
And raged with all the fires of war…

But winter is patient.

And when they returned weakened from the
effort,
She had her fun,
With hundreds of thousands.

# Secrets

We will never know their secrets,
That those brave men locked inside.
For they saw things no man should see.
They could not brush aside.

We will never know their secrets,
That those brave men locked inside.
For they witnessed too much death,
Talk risked their suicide.

We will never know their secrets,
That those brave men locked inside.
For they were taught of upper lips,
Had no one to confide.

We will never know their secrets,
That those brave men locked inside.
Their truth was never to be told,
In life or once they'd died.

We will never know their secrets,
That those brave men locked inside.
For they were judged by Homefront crowds,
That forced those men to hide.

# Forgotten

We have forgotten as they have forgotten,
Lost in lost minds,
We roam in deafening dins,
That silences us from ourselves.
We sit a line of strangers,
Until orders startle,
And we walk forwards forsaken,
By those who have forgotten.

# Regeneration

A generation lost.
Or so they like to say.

Cursed by death we were,
Our souls on lips that pray.

We were brave as we fought,
Heroes we fell each day.

Too bad it was for naught,
Our generation passed away.

And regeneration has lost,
Our time and sense and reason.

A new world filled with old,
Generations intent on treason.

They know not they cannot win,
When the bugles sound the season.

Our Great War's greater twin,
Will banish them from Eden.

# The Big Push

We heard rumours of the big push,
Quiet mutterings at first.
Whispers that shouted,
And stirred us from our sleep.

We knew the day was coming,
Trepidation shackled our thoughts,
As ladders arrived,
To make our climb to hell.

The orders came one morning,
Veiled in cold and dank mists,
That lay heavy as we stood in war,
And savoured it.

The calls soon came to fix bayonets.
Our hourglass was almost done,
As the front hushed a quiet,
A sigh before its end.

We consoled each other with small talk,
But ears were deafened to it.
For we were distracted by distractions,
That played with our senses. Our minds.

Then whistles whistled,
As wishes flew frightened.

We shared in that moment.
Glancing looks passed between dead men.

We climbed and clambered,
Over the top,
Struggling to our feet,
Weighted down by instinct.

We lost each other in the chaos,
And lost ourselves in the fight.
For the big push,
Had pushed too far this time.

# Death Sentence

I've been to the front.

Had tea with my executioner.

Who teases my passing.

Revels in my torment.

I'm its plaything.

To do with as it pleases.

A toy caged.

Until it gets bored.

And I'm not its plaything.

Anymore.

And when that time comes,

It will reveal itself to me,

And pass my death sentence,

For all,

And I,

To see.

# Conscripted

Cursed are those conscripts,
Conscripted to further the fight,
In a war that is not working,
A truth that's hidden from sight.

Packed off to the front like lambs,
Fresh meat to die at first light.
Young and old together,
As they whisper their final goodnight.

Cursed are those conscripts,
Conscripted to further the blight.
As they wallow in mud and fetid filth,
Ranks swollen enforced by invite.

Lied to their death like lemmings,
Who jump despite their sight,
Those poor souls have but one choice,
Trust God they'll be alright.

# If

If by some fortune I survive this,
And return home untainted.

I would like to kiss my darling sweetheart,
And meet my new-born babe,
As we shut our door to the outside,
And lock this war from our lives.


If by some miracle I should get through this,
And return home unchanged.

I would like to stand on the ground of fields,
And feel long grass caress my palms as I
run,
Back to the life I lived,
Before I left for war.


If by some chance I should see this to the
end,
And return home unaltered.

I would like to sit without flinching,
Sleep without warped dreams,
Both eyes shut to that world,
So that my soul can rest in peace.

If by some luck I should outlast this,
And return home unbroken.

I would live my life for every day,
And leave past and future alone,
For life is lived in the present,
But for now my present is war.

# Guilt

Guilt wears me down with memories,
Painful in their clarity that stab,
Prickly and sharp, like daggers,
Irritating in their torment.

They tease me from my sleep.
My invisible companion,
That stalks my dreams,
And conjures nightmares when I wake.

It reminds me with soundless whispers,
Hissing accusations that burrow into my
skull.
I can't shake it from my shoulder,
For it is clothed in my shame.

It sings to me when I'm alone.
Haunts conversations,
My everyday shadow,
That asks dreaded questions,

*How come you are breathing,*
*It starts,*
*When braver men, better men,*
*Lie breathless where they fell?*

I don't know.

*Unmarked save for poppies that keep their company,*
*And wilt before the sun.*
*Their petals fall like bodies,*
*Back to the mud.*

Please stop.
I hear it chuckle from deep inside.
It knows I would dig them from that mud,
Switch our places.

It laughs now.

How I have longed to exhume them,
Curse them with their life,
While I lie in their grave,
And bury myself with my guilt.

It laughs again,
And shows me more memories…

# Lest We Forget

Lest we forget that they walked through
bullet rains,
Stared down showering shells,
And breathed the gaseous winds,
That corrupted their eyes,
And dissolved their lungs,
Brought them agony,
Offered them death.
That hollowed mercy.

Lest we forget that they scarred in sight of
scars;
The bony chips that cut free from limbs,
As bloody waves pulsed from skulls,
Of mates digested by disease.
For that cruel war maimed them morbid,
Its reach seeping from their veins,
To birth a ruined form of life,
Familiar with the reaper's guises,
Fearing they'll be next.

Lest we forget that they fought for us,
The twinkling stars of unborn babes,
Of generations yet to be.
They struggled with sanity and snipers,
Shredded themselves on wire altars,
As shrapnel buried with them.

They sacrificed all that they were,
And handed us future.

Lest we forget that they fell in thousands,
And watched thousands fall before them,
As friends became strangers.
And madness had them fighting inside,
While they hunkered down in trenches,
Forgotten to their fate.

# The Great Pretend

We are all masked in ignorance,
For it is easier to ignore,
The truth,
That is our only backdrop,
As we dance on the stage.

Actors rehearsed in lies,
Who shoot at truth with bullets,
And die when they forget,
Their lines,
And characters.

Fools direct this theatre,
Affecting acts of their play.
We all know their folly,
But it is foolish to stand,
Against fools.

So we must proceed,
With scripted verse.
Our backs to the enemy,
Faces painted with smiles,
As we dance…

Until the curtain falls,
With the fools applause.
Then we warring thespians,

May cast off our costumes,
And throw down our roles and rifles.

For only then ends 'The Great Pretend'.

# Life Goes On

Life goes on or so I'm told.
Say that to those who survived the trenches,
And never returned.

Life goes on or so I'm told.
Say that to the crippled who limp in sad
shires,
That pretend they're not there.

Life goes on or so I'm told.
Say that to the widows shamed behind
doors,
Who grieve for answers buried with their
chaps.

Life goes on or so I'm told.
Say that to the broken caged in institutions,
That shock away their dignity.

Life goes on or so I'm told.
Say that to the grief stricken numbed to
carry on,
By heartless etiquettes and sad expectations.

Life goes on or so I'm told.
Say that to the survivors scarred by
memories,

Who wish the war had never been.

# Peace and Quiet

Peace and quiet. Is that what we fought for?
Did we lay down our lives,
And struggle like animals in their filth,
For peace?
For quiet?
For the things we already had,
Before the world went mad?

When the earth supped on a stew of bodies,
As we scrambled about like rodents,
Watching brothers break promises of return.
Was it for peace?
Was it for quiet?
How can it be right that they fell,
For the things war stole from them.

We now have our peace and our quiet,
But know that this world is never truly at
peace,
And the drums of war can be heard in that
quiet.
Drumming…
        Drumming…
                Drumming…
For the guns will one day break their
silence,
When boys fight for peace and for quiet,

All,

Over,

Again.

# An End to All That

I remember the day the guns stopped.
Deafening.
Silent.
Ringing doubt and hope in our ears,
Our minds.
The din of battles faded,
As men shot questions instead of bullets.
Small talk and idle chat.
Civilisation returned,
Animals went into hiding.

The news came quiet at first,
As if to hear its prized secret would make it
worthless,
Rifles would resume,
And guns would shoot the dove down.
But the news held steady that day.
A whisper at first,
To those who allowed themselves to
whimper,
And blubber as excitement bubbled to their
front.

Men slouched where they stood or sat,
As if the very sky had rested on their
shoulders all those years,
And now they were rid of it…

*Come to think of it the sky did seem higher…*
Brighter.
More magnificent that day.
Its beauty reflected in eyes that looked to it,
Those titans looking to the Gods.

Some shared a tear or two,
While others shared a smoke.
But we all allowed ourselves a pause,
To feel again.

We then laid down our guns,
As we were led out of trenches.
Our hands rid of their shame,
Eyes opening to the horrors.
Homeward bound we allowed one boot,
To lead the other out of hell.

For some of us this was just the beginning,
But for me it put an end to all that.

# Pals

Pals they were.
Pals they fell.
Pals together,
Beyond their knell.

Pals they signed.
Pals they trained.
Pals they battled,
When courage waned.

Pals each morning.
Pals each week.
Pals at Christmas,
Strong and meek.

Pals they fought.
Pals they shared.
Pals forever,
Lost or spared.

Pals they grieved.
Pals they stirred.
Pals they leant,
Shoulder and word.

Pals they lived.
Pals they died.

Pals in memory,
Forever with pride.

# Armistice

Doves fly from carriage clocks,
That had ticked away meaning,
As time recorded our folly.
Madness falls from minds then,
And the blind regain their sight.
An inky miracle,
Halting men from wetting the land,
That drank so greedily of their ink,
And supped on their damned signatures.
Reason and sanity long abandoned,
Return to relieved embraces,
That echo in armistice.
Lesser men sign for greater heroes,
Who reside in their wilderness. Still.
But the miracle calls to them,
And so the doves soar to mirrored heavens,
As bells sing the eleventh hour,
Heralding peace ascending in humbled
triumph,
As wearied masses rejoice in their sighs,
And feint lights fight back the dark,
To shine dimly on war,
With evanescence.

# 2018

One hundred years have passed.
And we who could never know.
Know nothing.
Of that Great War,
Of the passing of pals,
At each passing day.
Of the fear of passing on,
As loved ones passed before past eyes.

Eulogies have long escaped,
And echoed down the generations.
Speaking of their plight. Their plague.
But we choose to remember illusions,
That delude the disillusioned.

We care little of life.
Ignore death.
Their hard won freedoms,
Cast from hearts and minds,
And thrown to the dirt,
That those forsaken called home,
And fell in heavy rains,
And blinding sun,
And forceful winds.
The wrath of merciless natures.

Under stars and moonlight, cold and distant,

Silver beacons in the celestial glory of night
skies,
They lost and won,
Our everything.
They knew of life and what it meant to live.
And knew more of death and what it meant
to die.
And die they did.
But we who live in 2018,
Know little of life,
And even less of death.

For we are the ignorant. The petulant. The
self-obsessed.
A lost generation.
Whose feeds and pages,
Phones and consoles,
Soaps and dramas,
Sunday nights,
Holidays,
Clublands,
Booze –
Muddy muddled minds.

For we have forgotten,
The precious spoils of that Great War.
Of peace.
And humanity.
And reason.
History.

One hundred years have passed.

A bittersweet century.

And we who should know…

*Know nothing.*

15032425R00109

Printed in Great Britain
by Amazon